D1516536

CANDY STORE
© October 2010 Bella Andre

Chapter One

The orgasmic moans coming from behind Callie were too loud and impassioned for her to ignore any longer.

"Ooohh, I just died and went to heaven," exclaimed a middle-aged woman as she popped another truffle into her mouth. The teenager next to her said, "Stop hogging them all, mom," and reached across her mother to grab several treats off the tray the waiter was holding.

Callie smiled, pleased that everyone was enjoying the truffles so much, but then her smile turned into a frown as she remembered her accountant's words.

*Your business better start picking up,
and fast, or you're going to have to shut down
Callie's Candies.*

She slumped down in her seat with a
loud sigh. Her store wasn't bringing in enough
money to stay afloat. Even though everyone
who had ever tasted one of her confections
seemed to love them, she still wasn't able to
make ends meet. Her accountant had arranged
for her to meet with a renowned candy company
consultant on Monday, but right now Callie
wasn't feeling particularly hopeful about it. As
soon as anyone started talking about marketing
and promotion, Callie always started
daydreaming about new candy creations, no
matter how hard she tried to stay focused on
business plans.

She looked around the indoor garden at
the two hundred people who were munching on
her truffles with looks of utter rapture on their
faces and had to blink quickly to fight back a
sudden onslaught of tears.

How could she give up on Callie's
Candies? Making people happy was worth so
much more to her than making money, she
thought as she sniffled and opened her little
beaded purse to look for a tissue.

The woman behind her licked
bittersweet chocolate dust off of her fingers.

"Wait a minute, honey. I've got a tissue here in my purse for you. I always cry at weddings myself. Everything about them is so perfect and beautiful, isn't it?"

Callie forced herself to nod as she accepted the tissue from the woman. Ignoring the chocolate smear across it from the woman's fingers, Callie blew her nose.

She liked weddings. Really she did. Especially since the happy couple had met in her store last Valentine's Day.

She tucked the used tissue into her purse, trying hard to clear her mind. Right now she didn't want to think about Valentine's Day. She didn't want to think about weddings. And she sure as heck didn't want to think about love.

She snorted at the thought of love— didn't one need a boyfriend or even, say, a date first?—and the woman next to her scooted a little farther away.

Even a middle-aged stranger thought she was weird and wanted to get away from her. Callie reached for the used tissue and blew again.

The first few chords of the wedding march rang out and the guests leapt to their feet. Callie noted that everyone was either still chewing and swallowing or licking chocolate off of their fingers as they waited for the bride to appear.

She bit back a slightly hysterical laugh.

At least there's one thing about me that people love, she thought as the radiant bride stepped out from behind an arbor of white lattice and pink roses.

Too bad she couldn't barter chocolate truffles for love.

* * * * *

Derek stood next to the priest and tried not to sway. Planting his feet in a wide stance he clasped his hands behind his back and focused his eyes on the woman in white coming towards him.

Ruthless memories assaulted him. *What woman in her right mind would want to marry you? Candy is for children and I want a man.*

Everything blurred and Derek had to close his eyes to keep his feet firmly planted on the ground.

The priest leaned towards him. "This is a wedding, not a wake, son."

Derek forced a grin even though he thought his face might crack with the strain just as James, his best friend since the first grade, turned and gave him a thumb's up.

God, how he hated weddings. After his

one pathetic attempt at holy matrimony, which had ended before "I do" was done, Derek had vowed never to set foot within a mile of a wedding ever again.

And now, here he was, the best man. He knew he was a sucker, but when push came to shove he couldn't let James down. Missing his best friend's wedding would have been the coward's way out.

Derek was going to look his demons in the eye, support his friend on the happiest day of his life, and then get the fuck out.

Were it not for several quick swigs of tequila, he wouldn't have made it this far. And he knew damn well that several more shots would be necessary to help him get through the reception. It was the only way.

Jane's father kissed her on the cheek and handed the bride over to the groom. Derek saw the love flowing between them and felt nothing but emptiness inside him.

The memory tackled him again. *The Candy King? Why can't you be more like your brother?*

Derek tried to shake the shrill voice of his ex-fiancée out of his head as James and Jane exchanged rings. His best friend leaned in to kiss his new wife, but all Derek could see was the face of his ex-fiancée, screwed up in rage at him.

Don't ever come near me again.

In his mind's eye Derek could still see the shock on the faces of their guests. He could still see the undisguised hatred in Gina's eyes.

The sound of applause pulled him from his memories and he reached out his arm to the Maid of Honor. He just needed to make it down the aisle to the bartender and then everything would be all right.

* * * * *

Callie pushed the salmon around on her plate. It was delicious, but she wasn't the least bit hungry. Her lack of appetite may have had something to do with all of the newlyweds at her table. As far as she could tell there wasn't another singleton around for miles. If she had to hear one more word about engagement rings and honeymoon trips, she was going to puke. Abruptly, she pushed her chair back and made a beeline for the bar.

A tall, broad-shouldered man stood with his back to her. Callie hadn't paid much attention to the wedding ceremony, but she couldn't help but notice the striking good looks of the best man.

He had looked oddly grim throughout

the ceremony, but at one point when he had grinned at the groom, it was as if the sun had come out from the clouds to pour down over everyone.

Callie cursed her unfortunate weakness for tall, dark, and handsome. Her friends liked to joke that the big brutes she always fell for were the perfect counterpart to her petite curves. But it wasn't really all that funny.

The truth was that if the man came with a harsh past and an emptiness in his soul, she was metal to his magnet. Which may have had something to do with her still being single, she mused unhappily.

If she could only find a nice, simple, happy man—yes, short, soft, and pale would have to suffice—everything would be perfect.

Oh yeah, except for the fact that she was going to have to close her store if she didn't start making a profit.

Callie fell even deeper into her misery as she made her way past the last of the tables. The best man ran a large hand through his hair and said something in a low voice to the bartender. The sound of his voice sent goose bumps running up her bare arms.

I wonder which super model he's married to?

Callie knew she was being bad, but for

once she didn't care. Pretty soon, instead of spending her days making candy—the one thing she loved most in the world—she was going to be sitting behind a desk in an office typing memos for some executive, or reeking of grease and saying, "Would you like onions with that?"

Coming shoulder to shoulder with Mr. Handsome and Tortured, she said to the bartender, "Give me something. Anything. Just make it strong."

Alcohol wasn't normally her thing, not when she could do such amazing things with sugar and chocolate, but Callie didn't care.

If there was ever a time to get drunk, it was now.

The best man, who was even more striking up close, tossed back a shot of something golden then turned to face her.

"She'll have a shot of tequila," he told the bartender, all the while holding her gaze with his own. "Make it two. With lime and salt."

Callie had never seen eyes so green. She blinked and tried to tear her eyes from his, but she didn't have a chance.

"Derek McNear," he said, his voice warm and slightly thick.

Callie's tongue darted out to lick her lips. She knew she was supposed to say her name, but she was having the darnedest time even remembering to breathe around this guy. His name seemed vaguely familiar, but her brain wasn't working well enough for her to chase the thought.

One side of his mouth quirked up, but his semi-grin was far from being a smile.

"And you are?" he asked, his tone slightly mocking, as if he was used to women losing all use of their tongues whenever he deigned to speak to them.

The bartender placed a small glass in front of Callie and she finally pulled herself away from her trance of lust. It was long past time for her to stop acting like such an idiot. What did it matter how gorgeous this guy was?

He was probably married, she was definitely single, and that was that.

"Callie Moore," she said without looking at him again—god forbid she get stuck in those wicked green eyes again—and picked up the little glass. She took a small sip of the liquid and nearly spit it out.

Suddenly angry at being the butt of some stranger's joke, she turned towards the man, her eyes flashing.

"What is this? Are you trying to kill me?"

His laughter was so unexpected that Callie took a step back.

"Amazing. You've never had tequila before, have you?" he finally said, his words mixing with his laughter.

Callie shook her head, not trusting herself to say anything more to this awful, albeit incredible, specimen of a man. When he laughed his eyes lit up and she thought they sparkled like the ocean, which was a ridiculous thought given that the closest she'd ever come to seeing a green-blue ocean was during a documentary about Jacques Cousteau on television.

But before she could walk away— scratch that, run away—to her car and leave to go hide in her kitchen behind her store, he leaned down so that she could feel his warm breath across her cheek.

"Won't you let me show you how to make it taste good?"

His softly spoken words made shivers run all the way from the tips of Callie's breasts, which were now hard points of desire, past the vee of her legs, which was suddenly hot and aching, all the way down to the tips of her toes, which were fairly curling in her high heels. Every cell in her body was quivering in anticipation of whatever it was that Derek wanted to show her.

"Okay," came out in an exhale, wanting

him to show her far more than how to drink the
bitter beverage.

She would have been more shocked by
her response had she been able to think
remotely straight with this man invading her
personal space in such a seductive way.

He slid the two glasses together and
picked up a slice of lime. "First, you hold the
lime between your teeth, with the flesh facing
me."

Obediently, Callie opened up her mouth
and let Derek slide the small green fruit between
her lips. His thumb brushed lightly over her
bottom lip as he did so.

It struck her that he was touching her on
purpose to tease her with his power, to show her
that he already controlled her body with his
own. But she didn't care.

Not when just the slightest touch felt so
good.

"Tilt your neck to the side."

With hot, sure fingers, he brushed her
hair away from her neck and lightly pushed
aside the neckline of her long sleeve jersey
dress to bare a small patch of skin between her
neck and her collarbone.

Callie was about to burst with wanting
him. All he had done was touch her mouth and
her neck and she was about to explode into a

million pieces. She was shivering, but not with cold. It was a sunny day in the first week of January in frigid upstate New York, but Callie was burning up as if it was August in Barbados.

"Good. Very good," he said in a low voice, the tips of his fingers still upon her neck.

His soft words of approval – along with his touch – had Callie holding her breath, waiting for more.

"Now, I'm going to sprinkle a little salt onto your beautiful skin."

He shook several grains of salt onto her and Callie almost gasped aloud. She was, painfully, powerfully aware of the throbbing between her legs.

"Finally," he said, in so low of a voice she could barely hear him, "it's time for the tequila."

In one smooth motion, he leaned down and sucked at the skin on her shoulder, taking the salt into his mouth. Callie groaned with pleasure as his mouth seared her with its potent heat before he pulled back and downed the bitter liquid in the shot glass.

Callie was so mesmerized by his every move, his every breath, she was so under his spell, that she had forgotten all about the lime between her teeth until his mouth was a breath away.

He found her lips with the tip of his tongue, tasting every curve and the corners between her upper and bottom lips, taking his time to brand her before he sucked the juice from the lime.

If Callie had known limes could be so deliciously potent, she would have planted a row of fruit trees in her garden long ago and become a master of key lime pies.

Derek removed the lime from her mouth with his teeth. Dazed, she watched him pluck it from his mouth and put it in the empty shot glass. Loud clapping for the band playing at the reception was bringing Callie crashing back to reality, when he leaned down and said, "Your turn."

Callie stood dumbly, blinking at him. This gorgeous man actually thought she was going to lick salt from his neck and then suck a lime from his lips?

As if sensing her reservations, he said, "You don't want to waste your drink, now do you?"

What was she doing? She was a nice girl who owned a candy store, for god's sake. Not some wanton slut who picked up men at weddings.

She sneaked a glance down at his ring finger and breathed a sigh of relief. At least she wasn't a husband stealing slut.

And then, she remembered her store and how she was probably going to lose it. Suddenly, it was all too much for her to deal with.

"Oh, what the hell."

Chapter Two

Before she could change her mind, she picked up the slice of lime and shoved it rind-first into Derek's mouth.

He chuckled from around the lime and Callie's eyes narrowed as she looked up at him.

Was he laughing at her? The naïve little candy maker he was toying with at a wedding?

Well, she'd show him.

Blocking out any thoughts of where she was and how unseemly their drinking game was during the middle of a wedding reception, Callie focused on the task at hand.

To make Derek want her even more than she wanted him.

Oh yes, she was going to set him on fire and then leave him high and dry after she took what she wanted.

Coming up on her tippy-toes, she smiled coyly and ran her forefinger over the juice dripping from the lime onto his full lower lip.

"I didn't mean to be so rough with you," she said, bringing her finger to her mouth to suck the drop of juice dry.

His Adam's apple moved hard in his throat and his grin dropped away completely.

One point for team Callie.

She took her finger from her mouth and brought her hands up to the bow tie of his tux. "You've got an awful lot of clothes on, don't you?"

Derek raised an eyebrow. He couldn't speak around the lime in his mouth, but she could hear his silent challenge loud and clear: *"So what are you going to do about it?"*

Even with a slice of lime between his lips he looked daunting and powerful and far too sure of himself.

Callie forced herself to match his silent dare with a cheeky grin. Licking her lips, with great concentration she ran her small hands down the front of his tux, from his broad shoulders, down past his well-formed pecs, to what she assumed was a washboard stomach.

Even as insecurity reached in to her bravado, she made herself take one of his lightly calloused hands in her own. She ran the tip of her finger along the soft skin and muscle at the curve between his thumb and forefinger and smiled with pleasure at his fast, hard exhale. Her heart beating way too fast, she slowly turned his hand over and continued tracing the skin on his palm.

More turned on than she'd ever been before—even though she was in public with a man she'd known for five minutes—Callie pushed the sleeve of his tuxedo jacket up to his forearm.

Barely able to keep her fingers steady, Callie undid the gold cufflink from his dress shirt and let it drop to the floor. Slowly, precisely, she folded his starched sleeve up once, then twice. Every time her fingertips brushed against his, heat surged through her.

Derek's pulse beat rapidly under the exposed skin of his wrist. She wanted to cover his heartbeat with the heat of her mouth.

"Perfect," she breathed, the spell remaining unbroken as she reached for the salt and sprinkled it on to his tanned wrist and the edge of his palm.

Raising his wrist to her mouth, Callie paused in a beat of delicious anticipation before dropping her lips to his skin.

She groaned as she sucked at him, hardly tasting the salt, desperate for a taste of his essence, so potent and male and wonderful. Unwilling to lose contact with him, she licked a grain of salt off of the firm flesh on his palm.

A low sound came from deep in his throat, like he was a caged lion on the verge of escape.

Silently promising herself his mouth if she could tear her lips away from his wrist, Callie reached for the shot glass and drank the tequila in one long swallow.

This time it wasn't bitter and she didn't think it was going to kill her. Instead it made her feel warm, even warmer than she already was, and languid and perfect.

And then, she got back up on her tippy-toes and placed her hands behind Derek's neck. She threaded her fingers into his soft hair and he leaned into her so that she could place her teeth around the lime in his mouth.

She sucked the juice from it without ever touching her skin to his, and then suddenly the lime was gone and he was kissing her, conquering her, showing her that if she was going to play, they were going to play the game by his rules.

As his strong hands encircled her back, she felt safe and hot and scared and wet and she wanted to curl up inside Derek and never come out.

"Ahem." The bartender cleared his throat. "I think the bride and groom are trying to get your attention."

Callie heard the bartender from within a thick fog of lust, but she wanted to ignore it, if hearing him meant leaving heaven.

It was Derek who finally pulled away. With one last heavy look, his devil-may-care grin was back on his face.

Everything hit her at once, and Callie felt as if she had been thrown from a hot tub to a ice cold plunge with no warning.

Worse, everyone at the wedding – plenty of potential customers among them - had just witnessed her throwing herself at a stranger.

Obviously guessing her thoughts, Derek leaned in and whispered, "No one could see you behind me. There's nothing to worry about."

Unable to meet his eyes, she turned and ran blindly away from the gathering, instinctively heading for the one place that she would feel safe again—the kitchen.

She darted through the swinging door and stepped to the left just in time to avoid a collision with one of the waiters. Her eyes wild, she ran past the prep area, past the stoves, rounded a corner and found refuge in the walk-in refrigerator. Stepping inside, she slumped down onto an upside down milk crate and tried to catch her breath.

She was just going to have to hide in the

refrigerator until the reception was over.

Chapter Three

"May the bride and groom have true love forever!"

Derek raised his champagne glass in a toast to James and Jane, doing his best to act the part of the happy best man, when all he could think about was the little vixen who had just run away from him.

"Has anyone seen Callie?" Jane asked after the endless toasts were through. At her guest's blank stares, she added, "She made the incredible truffles."

People moaned with remembered pleasure and licked their lips and said things like, "Better than sex," and "Are there more?"

Derek smiled. He should have known that Callie had something to do with candy. Candy was, after all, his specialty. And Callie was so damn sweet, especially her plump lips and the succulent patch of skin at the base of her neck. He couldn't wait to taste the rest of her, to run his tongue over every inch of her body, from her lush breasts and her taut nipples, which he was guessing were a dusty rose on the creamy skin of her breasts, to the valley between her thighs, and…

Jane's voice cut through his X-rated daydream. "Darn. I wish she was here so I could officially thank her, well, for everything." Jane reached for her new husband's hand. "If it weren't for Callie's Candies, James and I would have never found each other."

James leaned over and frenched his newly wedded wife. Derek shifted from one foot to the other in discomfort and looked away. *Get a room,* he thought, but then, he had just been about to lay Callie out on top of the bar, so who was he to complain?

When his best friend was finally done kissing his bride, he turned towards Derek with a knowing grin. "Any idea where Callie might be?"

"Not a clue," Derek answered truthfully. "But I'd be happy to go find her for you."

"I bet you would," James said with a wink. "For us."

Glad to be free of his best man duties, Derek headed for the door Callie had run through.

"Did anyone see a woman run through here?"

One of the waiters nodded towards the hall behind the prep area and the stoves. "She went back there."

Derek nodded his thanks. Once he had walked around the corner into the hidden, back area of the kitchen, he saw two large doors, both big enough for him to step through. Opening the door to his right, he realized it was a commercial freezer, packed full of ice cream containers and huge bags of ice.

He closed the heavy freezer door and turned his gaze to the refrigerator door, a broad grin taking over his face. He almost felt sorry for his hot little candy maker.

She may have intended on cooling off in the fridge, but he was going to make sure that she got a hundred times hotter instead.

* * * * *

Callie heard a noise in the hall and looked up through the thick, frosted glass on the refrigerator door. A tall man in a tux was standing just outside the door.

"Oh no."

She tried to push herself back further

into the shelves, hoping that her dark pink dress would help her to blend in with the crates of supplies. Maybe if she didn't move, didn't make a sound, didn't even breathe, he would go away. And she could be left in peace with her memory of the taste of his skin and the beating of his heart on her lips.

Callie had spent the past ten minutes rubbing the goose bumps on her arms and trying to convince herself that she had had enough of Derek. She didn't need to see him, didn't need to touch him, didn't need any more of his kisses.

But now that he was standing only feet from her—somehow she had known all along that he would find her and now he had—it was all she could do not to fling the door open, pull him inside the cramped space with her, and rip his clothes off.

Who was she kidding? She wasn't going to be content with just the memory of him, with just her dreams of what it would be like to feel him naked against her, writhing in pleasure.

At the same time, an annoying inner voice of reason was telling Callie there was no point to giving in to her baser needs. One night of mind-blowing sex wasn't going to help anything. It wasn't going to save her business.

And it wasn't going to save her pathetic

love life.

Although, she thought with a small upturn of her lips, it was guaranteed to be fun.

The doorknob turned and she stood up and backed into the wall, pressing herself back against the cold edge of the laden shelves as far as she could.

In the dim light of the refrigerator, Derek's warm voice wrapped around her.

"I thought I might find you in here."

Callie was both alarmed and aroused by his presence, by the way he filled up the room with his essence. The crazy mix of feelings made it hard for her to speak. Again.

"I, uh…" she said as he stepped into the refrigerated space with her.

Less than four feet from her, which was at least four feet too close for Callie's comfort, he closed the door behind him with a soft but definite click, never once taking his eyes from her.

His voice laced with humor, he said, "There's no lock, but at least it's private. We'll just have to hope no one needs any milk."

Looking for a way out, for some sort of escape path, willing herself to think fast so that she could get the heck away from him, she said, "Actually, I was looking for the milk, for, um, coffee for the reception." Picking up a carton of milk, she said, "So now that I've found it, I…"

Derek took a step towards her and Callie, who felt as if she was the lioness being hunted by a needy lion, dropped the carton of milk on the floor. It broke open and spilled onto her shoes, but she hardly noticed the wet splash of milk.

All she could feel was his heat, as if he was drawing him to her via some sort of sexual infrared.

She could try all day, all week, all year, to tell herself she didn't want what he was offering her. But it would never stop being a lie. Because she did need it. Because she did need him.

Desperately.

He pinned her against the shelves with one arm on either side of her. "You weren't looking for milk," he said, his voice husky. "You were looking for this."

He captured her mouth in a kiss so sweet, so powerful, that Callie was instantly infused with a deep warmth. He nipped at her lips, biting softly at the sensitive, cool flesh, burning her up as his fingers made quick work of her dress by hiking it up around her waist,

Thanking god she hadn't been able to find a pair of nylons without a run in it, she lost what was left of her breath as Derek's fingers made their way up the naked flesh of her inner thigh, teasing her with their intent.

He pulled one of her legs up and, breathless with anticipation, Callie felt herself grow more and more swollen, until finally he pushed past the wispy silk of her panties and found her slick and ready and wet.

Callie pushed herself into his hand, no more able to stop herself from grinding into him than she would have been able to walk away and leave.

And all the while, as the hard flesh of his palm aroused her clitoris until she almost hurt with it, Derek drove her crazy with his gentle kisses.

Callie had always been perfectly happy to let men lead in bed, content to let her lovers take their time exploring her. But if she didn't get more of Derek this very second—his mouth, his hands, the huge, hard shaft that was pressing against her palm as she cupped his heavy weight through his black tuxedo pants—she was going to die.

She plunged her tongue into his mouth and found his, forcing it to mate with hers. He growled his pleasure and she matched it with her own moan.

Lifting his mouth from hers, Derek reached for the jersey fabric of her dress. "I need to see you," he said in a low voice.

Callie pulled her dress up over her head then reached for Derek's jacket, roughly yanking it off of his shoulders.

"I need to taste you," she said as she ripped off his bow tie and jerked his shirt open at the neck, and then her lips and tongue found the hollow of his neck, found his strong, quick pulse.

He slid his hands to her back, stroking flames onto her skin, and then her bra was on the floor, and his sure fingers overtook hers, clumsy with cold and need as she tried to remove his shirt.

Knocking off several cartons of milk from a low shelf beside them, he propped her up on it. Callie reached for his belt, but he had already dropped to his knees, his mouth at her breasts, licking and sucking at the soft, plump flesh, coming closer and closer to her nipples, but not nearly close enough.

Already puckered from the refrigeration, her areolas tightened into tiny buds of bliss as he licked slow circles around them, almost flicking against her nipples, but never quite touching them.

"Please," Callie moaned, her hands wound into Derek's thick, dark hair, her head thrown back, her back arched. She pushed herself into him, any remaining vestiges of modesty gone, impatient for him to put her out of this exquisite agony.

"Not yet," he said, taking her ample breasts into his hands. Reverently, he ran his thumbs lightly over her nipples, then back again, flicking the tight buds with his fingers.

"Dusty rose. I knew it," he said softly as he worshiped her. His mouth consumed her as he tasted every square inch of her glorious breasts, rising up from her rib cage to the taut peak of her nipples. "You're so beautiful. So damn beautiful."

Callie had always been more than a little embarrassed by the size of her breasts—D cups on a five foot frame had always seemed way out of proportion—but if Derek continued to lick and suck her like that, she vowed to never have another bad thought about them again.

"Oh god, yes," she whimpered, her sounds of pleasure muffled by the thick walls of the refrigerator.

She was so hot, burning up everywhere he touched her. And then his hands were lifting her up and pulling her panties off, the wispy silk scratching the sensitive skin on her inner thighs. Her panties fell to her ankles and she kicked them off.

And then, suddenly, shockingly, Derek's

head was between her legs, his tongue on her.

Gasping with surprise – and pleasure so dark and deep it threatened to pull her under – she instinctively opened her legs up wider and bucked her hips up into his mouth as he lightly touched the tip of her clit, engorged and so sensitive.

He held her firmly away from his mouth, lapping at her once, then twice, then blowing lightly on her heated flesh.

"More," she cried, no longer worried about anyone walking in on them, no longer caring if anyone in the kitchen heard her scream out for him.

A smile on his lips, he reached for her and brought her lips to his, letting her taste her juices, letting her lick them from his tongue.

"You have the sweetest pussy," he said, just as she begged, "Please, Derek."

His hand on her thigh, only inches from her lips, he said, "I like hearing my name on your lips. Say it again."

"Dere-"

He was kissing her before she got to the k. "Now tell me what you want me to do to you."

She didn't even have to think. "Lick me again."

He moved down and licked her kneecap.

"Here?" he asked, his eyes devious and challenging.

"No," she cried, wishing he would give her what she wanted, wishing he wouldn't make her say the words.

He licked the tender flesh on the inside of her elbow.

"Here, sweetheart?"

She gave in, need pushing her all the way off the ledge of fear. Of whatever propriety she had left.

"My pussy," she whispered, amazed to hear the word roll off her tongue.

"Lick my pussy," she said again, her voice louder, more sure as she realized how much she liked the feel of the word as it rolled from her tongue to her lips and then out into the cold air of their private refrigerated world.

He kissed her hard on her lips, bruising them, before kissing a trail down her flesh, from the hollow of her neck to the valley between her lush breasts.

"I," he pulled at her nipples with his mouth, causing shivers of ecstasy to race down her spine, "would be happy," his tongue dipped into her belly button, "to lick," and then lower still to the very tip of her clit, "your pussy again."

And then his mouth was on her, hot and

insistent. His tongue plunged in and out of her canal, he sucked on her swollen clit, and Callie cried out as all of the pressure that had been building up since she first saw Derek standing at the bar threatened to explode into a million glorious pieces. Impossible tremors wracked her, knocking her back against the shelves, pushing her off the counter into his lips and teeth and hands.

He slipped one finger into her slick, pulsing canal, then two, and Callie felt her muscles clench around him, trying to take him even deeper. Envisioning his cock pumping in and out of her, just like his fingers were doing, rough and powerful and perfect, her heart started pounding so hard, so much faster than she thought it could, and she came apart completely for him.

Chapter Four

On his knees, sticky in a pool of milk, Derek could hardly think. Hell, he could hardly breathe.

He was no stranger to sweaty, grinding sex, but he couldn't help but be amazed by what happened to him with Callie.

He got within five feet of her and he lost his mind. He had to have her. Every perfect inch of her.

She was heedless in her passion, shy yet demanding, hungry for his touch, yet waiting for him to make the next move.

His cock throbbed in his pants, demanding attention. With his free hand, he undid his belt buckle and unzipped his pants and slipped on a condom he'd stashed in his wallet. Steadying Callie, who had leaned her weight against him as she recovered from the orgasm that had ripped through her, Derek slowly slid his fingers from her, pressing one last kiss to her sweet cunt, licking her sweet juices off of his lips before he rose up from his knees.

He looked down at the tip of his throbbing cock resting at her incredibly wet, pink entrance, the swollen head red with insistence, and wanted to plunge into her, roughly, forcefully, until he exploded. He wanted to feel her gorgeous breasts heavy in his hands as he rode her.

Dominating her, body and soul.

He wanted to grab her ankles and push them over his shoulders, opening up her thighs wide so that both of them could watch his cock sink into her, stretch her sweet flesh, inch by inch.

But even though he wanted to do all of this and more, he didn't. Because even more than Derek wanted to take Callie for his own pleasure, he wanted to please her all over again.

More than anything, he wanted to hear her cries of ecstasy, he wanted the pleasure of watching her come apart again beneath him.

Quickly slipping on a condom he'd stashed in his wallet, he looked into beautiful blue eyes, so shy again, and he opened his mouth to murmur something comforting to her, to let her know that she was safe with him, that he was going to take his time, even if it killed him, but then her eyes changed, turning from a clear ocean to a swirling, deep dark blue.

Before he knew it, she was bucking her hips into him.

"Callie," he groaned against her lips.

She shut him up with a kiss so full of ownership, Derek had a flash of knowledge that would have stunned him had he been able to get past the wet heat of her around his cock.

He would be hers forever.

Bucking and rearing, he slid in and out of her, delirious with pleasure. Her full breasts struck his chest with every thrust and her kisses sucked all of the breath from his lungs.

Barely coherent, Derek felt her muscles begin to tighten around his shaft. Mustering what little control he had left, he held her ass still with his big hands.

"Look at me."

As if from a dream, Callie opened her eyes slowly. Hazy with passion, she watched him watch her. He slid out one inch, and then another.

Her eyelids fell shut and he stilled again. "Open your eyes."

Slowly she re-opened them and he thought he saw defiance in their depths.

"They're open. Now show me a good time."

Derek would have laughed if he could have. Instead he thrust into her so hard that bottles fell from the shelf onto the floor, barely missing them as her eyes change again from a deep blue to a dark purple. Her nails dug into his back as her orgasm overtook her and it was all he could do not to shout out as he threw his head back, and came hard and long.

Finally, when the earth stopped shaking beneath his feet, he realized Callie's body language had changed beneath him. It might have been an imperceptible change to some men, but Derek recognized it immediately for what it was.

Embarrassment.

And shame.

No.

No way.

He tried to capture her mouth in a kiss, but she turned her head to the side and his lips grazed her cheek, instead. She wriggled her butt cheeks back into the shelves behind her and pushed at his chest.

He fell out of her and she moved quickly, reaching for her bra and her dress. She threw them over her head and Derek, figuring he'd have a better chance of reasoning with her if he had some clothes on too, quickly dressed back into his now-wrinkled, slightly milky tuxedo.

Loud voices sounded from the hall just as Callie put her hand on the doorknob. "Stay in here until everyone is gone. I'll distract them."

Derek frowned. He didn't want to embarrass Callie by giving away his presence, but at the same time, he couldn't let her get away.

"Wait for me," he said, but she was already out the door and gone.

Sitting down on an upside-down milk crate, Derek rubbed his eyes with the heel of his palms. Her scent was everywhere on him.

"She's not going to get away," he promised himself as he looked around at the mess they'd made in the commercial refrigerator.

Who knew a refrigerator could be so damn hot?

Chapter Five

The next morning, Derek's smile lit up the cloudy winter's day. He planned to check in at his office, have his assistant clear his schedule, and then he was going to track down Callie Moore.

Sweet, delectable Callie Moore.

Derek walked past the *Sweet Returns: Candy Company Consultant* sign and into his office building in downtown Albany, New York.

Alice, his assistant, had already been hard at work for several hours, writing up invoices, balancing his accounts, keeping everything running so smoothly that all he ever had to do was think about the best ways to sell candy.

"The king has finally arrived," she said, her mouth tight as she glanced towards the clock.

Alice had managed his office since the day he'd hung out his shingle fifteen years ago and often treated him like he was no more than an unruly kid who needed a ruler taken to his backside every once and again to stay on the straight and narrow.

"And not a minute too soon. You need to read through several things before you meet with your new client."

Derek sat down in a chair, guilt momentarily weighing him down. How was he ever going to let Alice go? When he closed up his candy consulting business and joined his older brother, Ed, in the accounting firm next month, Alice was going to be heartbroken. Not to mention disapproving.

The smile reappeared on his face. Alice loved to disapprove of whatever it was he did. Riling her up was part of the fun of working with her.

Promising himself he'd sit down and have a talk with her soon, he pushed it from his mind. "I need you to clear my calendar for the day." And hopefully for the next month or so, Derek thought.

He was already envisioning a trip to the Hawaiian Islands with Callie wearing nothing but a string bikini on a hot, sandy beach. Long days in the sun, followed by perfect nights under the stars. With Callie.

Adorable, sensuous Callie.

Cutting into his fantasy, Alice said, "No can do. You have an important consultation today." Her voice was full of censure. Derek wondered if she had used x-ray powers to guess his most intimate thoughts.

He was firm. "Cancel it."

"I can't and I won't. The woman I spoke to sounds sweeter than sweet, truly in love with making candy, and, most importantly, desperately in need of your help."

Derek frowned at Alice, then got up out of the leather chair and stalked to her desk.

"Fine." He reached his hand out for the packet of client information. "I'll go."

He grabbed the file without looking at it, impatient and displeased that he wasn't going to be able to go see Callie right away. Who cared about selling candy when what waited for him was so much better than any saltwater taffy, sour ball, or chocolate bar could ever be?

"Who's the client?"

"Callie's Candies."

Derek nearly dropped the folder. "Did you just say Callie's Candies?"

A curious glint in her eyes, Alice nodded. "That's right. My sister lives in Saratoga with that horse-crazy husband of hers and last time I went out to visit her, we dropped into Callie's Candies. Best damn truffles I ever had."

"I know," Derek said, remembering the rapturous faces of the wedding guests as they ate Callie's truffles. They had the same look that was currently drawn across Alice's face.

"I've never seen you get so excited about candy before," he said, teasing his assistant.

"There are a lot of things you haven't seen," she snapped at him as if he wouldn't know up from down without her help. Returning to an all-business demeanor she said, "She's expecting you at 10 a.m. Don't be late. And don't you dare let her down."

Intent on finding out everything he could about Callie's Candies before 10 a.m., Derek stepped into his office and closed the door. Opening the thick file of information that Alice had assembled for him, he started reading.

* * * * *

Callie's alarm went off at 7 a.m. and she burrowed down under the covers, trying to ignore it. She felt like hell today, which was no wonder, considering she'd barely slept all night. Her dog, Wolf, got up from his doggy bed on the floor and pushed his chin up on her pillow.

Feeling the weight of his big, shaggy head hit the bed, she emerged from beneath the down duvet. "All right, I hear you. I'm turning it off."

Silence descended again and she was certain she heard Wolf sigh with relief.

She sat up in bed and scratched Wolf's head between his ears. Just like she knew he would, he got so relaxed that his head slid off the bed and he stretched out on the rug beside her bed to go back to sleep.

The sheets scratched the tender skin of her breasts and Callie lightly ran her hands over them, a potent reminder of what she had done at James and Jane's wedding only a day before.

All night long, images of her coming in Derek's mouth, of his teeth grazing her shoulder as he sucked salt from her, of him thrusting into her while she clawed at his shoulders, assailed her.

How could she have behaved like that? She hadn't even recognized herself in the woman she had become yesterday in his arms. All she wanted to do was put a closed sign on the door of her candy store and stay under the covers until the memories finally went away.

Unfortunately, that wasn't possible. Not only did she have potential customers to sell candy to—not enough, of course, but the ones who came were loyal and she loved each and every one of them—but she had an important business meeting.

Her accountant had set up an appointment for her with a renowned candy company consultant, Sweet something or other was the name of his company. He was going to be coming by her store at 10 a.m.

No matter how she felt today, she couldn't miss this meeting, or she'd really be screwed. Literally and figuratively.

She dragged herself out of bed, almost stepping on one of Wolf's big mutt paws. She bent over to drop a kiss on his muzzle in apology and then stepped into the shower. She turned it on full blast, praying that water could wash away some of her sins.

Roughly soaping up her skin, she lathered up her arms, her legs, her stomach, trying to avoid the inside of her thighs until the last minute. She didn't want to touch herself, had held off from touching herself all night, even though her every waking moment had been filled with arousing images of her and Derek at the bar and in the refrigerator.

Her short dreams when she had fallen asleep had been even worse than that. After only a few minutes of sleep she woke up, drenched in sweat, the apex of her legs—she couldn't believe she had actually said the word pussy yesterday—throbbing with need.

But the need Derek unleashed in her was so great that her hands had a mind of their own. Before she knew it she was touching herself, rubbing herself, pretending that Derek's tongue was on her again.

Her clit grew huge and hard and her legs were trembling so badly that she had to lean back against the wall for support. She imagined him in the shower with her, her legs wrapped around his waist, his cock driving into her, his strong arms supporting her weight, his tongue in her mouth.

The orgasm hit her like a city bus and nearly knocked her down. She rubbed herself frantically, not wanting the tremors to end, not wanting the fantasy of Derek being with her to be erased when she opened her eyes.

When she'd shampooed her hair and dried off, working to push all erotic thoughts away, Callie dressed in the most severe outfit she owned, a light pink suit. Underneath the jacket, she wore a silk camisole.

She didn't intend to take her jacket off for the meeting—the suit was more like armor than clothes in her mind—and the white silk looked the best of anything she owned peeking out from underneath her jacket. Callie usually wore jeans and a t-shirt that said Callie's Candies on it, so today she felt business-like and stern in her suit.

Wolf followed her out of the bedroom and she let him into her little fenced backyard to take care of his business.

"I'll come back at lunch," she called to him and he turned his furry face to hers, wagging his tail as if he understood.

Downtown Saratoga, home to the famous horse races, was only ten minutes from her cottage. It had snowed the night before, but by 8 a.m. the streets were nicely plowed and the sidewalk slush had melted.

Callie had spent her whole life in Saratoga, but the Saratoga of today was very different from the town she knew so well as a child. When Callie was a little girl, she used to ride her bike into town with her friends, fifty cents in her pocket, straight to the candy store. They'd fill up their bags with jujubes and Necco wafers and jawbreakers and then head to the park and stuff themselves full of sugar under an elm tree. As a teenager, when Callie realized she had been blessed with the gift of candy making, she knew that, as soon as she could, she would open up her own candy store on Main Street.

Her dream became a reality when she

was twenty-five years old. She had saved every penny from her various cooking and catering jobs over the years, only spending the bare minimum on her cottage, and all of the sweat and grease was worth it when she signed the lease for her very own candy store.

The first time she walked by the vacant storefront that was now Callie's Candies, the old rundown ice cream shop didn't look like much good for anything other than for breeding spiders and mice. Narrow but deceptively long, with a large kitchen in back, it was covered in dust and neglect.

But for Callie, it was her first brush with true love. She immediately envisioned the space a buttery yellow, glass display cases full of truffles and fudge, old wine barrels on the floor with fresh, homemade saltwater taffy.

The past five years had been the most rewarding time of her life. She made candy in the evening and sold it by day. She loved watching the glee on the children's faces as they flew in off of their bikes, strewn haphazardly on the wide sidewalk, anticipation glowing in their eyes.

They knew that Miss Callie would always give them free samples of whatever she had just made that day, whether it was vanilla swirl fudge or chocolate turtle pie. And even

when they pulled a dollar out of their dirty
shorts and handed it to her for a bag of taffy,
they couldn't wait to get outside and see what
little "extra" Callie had thrown in for them,
maybe a lollipop or a wax-paper-covered slice
of fudge.

If they were really lucky, and they had
been given money from their mothers for a box
of truffles to take home, Callie gifted them with
a handful of lollipops and gummy worms.

But now that popular chain stores ruled
the street along with swanky restaurants and
wine bars, Callie's rent had doubled, then
tripled in the past five years. With every year,
she found it harder and harder to put something
away in the bank after she had paid her bills.
People were always telling her to put up a
website and advertise, but she didn't know the
first thing about that kind of stuff.

And she didn't want to. She just wanted
to make candy and watch the joy on her
customers' faces as they ate it.

Callie pulled into the plowed parking lot
behind her building, then walked through the
narrow alley between buildings to the sidewalk.
She always made it a point to enter her store by
the front door in the morning. Her first sight of
the pretty yellow, blue, and white striped
awning over the window and the fanciful

cartoonish painted letters of Callie's Candies on the flag beside the door made her incredibly happy.

She unlocked the front door and walked in, pulling up the shade on the door, scanning the glass for smudges or smears. Satisfied that it was clear and clean, she headed for the back room, breathing in the scent of sugar and cocoa powder, feeling settled for the first time since the wedding the day before.

Her store didn't open until 11 a.m., Monday through Friday, but Callie always had plenty to do in the morning. The best was making fudge or coating truffles in coconut and peanuts. The worst was going through her inventory and doing her orders for the week.

This was inventory day, of course. Callie sighed with dismay. Today of all days, she could have used a long, therapeutic session with some caramel and nougat.

"Figures," she muttered, as she walked into her small office at the back of the store and put her purse down. She took off her suit jacket and laid it across the back of her desk chair. Unbound by the jacket, her breasts felt free and immodest in the white lace camisole, reminding her yet again of her wanton behavior at the wedding.

"Forget about it. You've got work to

do," she lectured herself and got straight to it, intent on ignoring the new sensual sensations her body was sending her.

Picking up her clipboard and supply spreadsheet, she went to her dry storeroom first and noted what was low. Moving to her walk-in refrigerator, she checked materials off her list from the top shelf first. The bottom shelves were deep and she had to get on her knees to count cocoa bars. The position was awkward, with her rear end pointing straight up, her hands and knees sprawled unladylike on the floor.

For the past five years, Callie had planned on putting in sliding shelves on the bottom of her refrigerator. Unfortunately, the project never made it to the top of her ever-growing to-do list so she hadn't gotten to it quite yet.

Squirming around, trying to get comfortable in her clumsy position, she said, "One, two, three, four," aloud as she counted stacks of the finest imported cocoa bars.

Immersed in her counting and in the painful crick that was building up in her neck, she was surprised by footsteps coming up the short hallway and then stopping at the doorway to her storeroom.

"We've got to stop meeting in refrigerators like this."

Chapter Six

Callie's heart almost stopped beating. She would have recognized that smooth, deep voice anywhere.

She froze in place, unable to get her limbs to work. She couldn't believe that Derek's first image of her outside of the wedding refrigerator was like this—could she be any less sexy, she wondered dejectedly—in her own damn commercial refrigerator.

Her face, she was sure, was going to be flushed a deep shade of red when she finally stood up, considering that the man she had been lusting after for the past twenty-four hours had walked into her store unannounced, just in time to witness her pawing through her shelves on her hands and knees with her butt sticking straight up in the air.

"On second thought," he said, his voice

washing over her like hot caramel, "I think I like it."

For a millisecond, Callie considered trying to crawl onto the shelf, hoping that Derek would just go away. Then again, she thought, she hadn't invited him to her store. In fact, she hadn't even told him she had a store, so how could it possibly be her fault that he had found her looking less than ideal?

Trying desperately to rouse up some anger—otherwise she was stuck with embarrassed and horny, and that was a terrible combination—Callie crawled backwards and stood up, brushing invisible specks of dust off her knees and skirt.

Her arms folded across her chest, she said, "What are you doing here?"

Derek was leaning against the door, looking more gorgeous than any man had a right to in his pin-striped shirt and well-tailored coat and slacks.

He grinned and Callie wanted to smack the smile from his lips.

She also wanted to kiss him senseless, of course, but she was going to have some control over herself if it killed her.

Which it probably would.

"This is Callie's Candies isn't it?"

Callie nodded, keeping her lips firmly

pressed together, forcing herself to back up into the refrigerator shelves, rather than jump Derek's bones.

"I'm here for our appointment."

"Our appointment?"

She was utterly mortified, sure that her skin was turning pinker and pinker by the second. If things got any worse, she would fade away completely into the fabric of her pink suit.

"10 a.m., Monday morning. My assistant set it up with your accountant."

"You can't be the guy who-" She shook her head. "That's impossible, because-"

She leaned her weight into the cool air of the refrigerator as the full ramifications of her actions came crashing down upon her.

"Oh god."

Thoughts rushed around her brain, knocking into each other as the magnitude of her mistake sunk in.

She'd slept with the Candy King.

She'd had a one-night stand with the one person who could save her business.

What if he thinks I knew who he was all along and did it on purpose?

Struggling to sound like she had at least half a handle on her life, she said, "Please forgive me. You're with Sweet…"

Callie let her voice drop and looked up

towards the ceiling as if she obviously knew the name of his company but had momentarily forgotten it. She hoped against hope that he would fall for her act.

The truth was, she was such a bad business owner she didn't even know the name of the company that had been sent in to save her from ruin.

"Sweet Returns," he said smoothly, his eyes running past her flushed face to her chest, then quickly back up to her face.

Too late Callie realized that she was flashing Derek through the translucent white silk of her flimsy camisole. She crossed her arms across her chest, wanting to hide her telltale arousal, but it was no use.

With her arms crossed beneath her breasts, the soft flesh rose indecently up out of the v-neck top of her skimpy shell. She didn't know which was worse: her hard, pink nipples shooting through the fabric like darts, or the bounteous mounds of her breasts spilling from her top.

Wishing she weren't always doing the wrong thing at the wrong time, Callie bit her lip and said, "Should we get down to business?"

But no matter how hard she tried to act professional, Callie knew she sounded like she'd rather get kissed by Derek than look at the bottom line with him.

She couldn't help it. Derek was so damn gorgeous. And sexy. And…

Standing right in front of her.

With the intimacy that comes from knowing just how a woman needs to be touched, he brushed back a curl from her cheek.

Callie shivered.

Just like the visions that had kept her awake all night long, Derek was right there within stroking distance. She needed him so desperately that against any good sense she had ever possessed, her arms uncrossed and moved across his shoulders to entwine around his neck and she pressed her breasts up against his hard chest.

"Callie."

His voice wrapped around her like a deep fog, husky and full of the very need she herself was unable to fight, and then his mouth was on hers and her lips were open and greedy and she was moaning. He felt so good, so damn good, she was nearly sobbing with need.

He sucked at her lower lip, letting his teeth graze her skin, still sensitive from their lovemaking at the wedding, before moving his mouth down past her chin to the side of her neck.

"I was awake all night dreaming about

doing this again. Touching you again. Loving you again."

He sank his lips into the crook of her neck and sucked at it.

"Me too," she admitted on a gasp of pleasure, unable to stop the confession from rolling off of her tongue.

He hooked his thumb under the strap of her sheer camisole and slid it off one shoulder, baring the top of her breast.

Callie felt her nipples jut out even further, heard herself crying out his name as she let her neck fall back and pressed her breasts into his eager mouth.

In five seconds flat she forgot everything – that she was a good girl, that she hardly knew him, that she was the kind of woman who had a good time in an actual bed, not standing in her storeroom. All she cared about was the feel of his lips and tongue and teeth on her breasts, the way his light stubble felt sandy against her soft skin, the way his hands were cupping her butt cheeks, molding her hips into his hardness like he owned her.

She yanked his jacket off of his shoulders and threw it on the floor as her tongue mated frantically with his. Needing to touch his naked skin more than she needed to breathe, she pulled his shirt out from his pants, finally sighing with pleasure when her fingers found the warm, rippling muscles on his back.

With his foot, Derek slammed the door shut and spun them around, pressing Callie up against it. She felt his hardness, still covered by his wool slacks, press into her panties, which were already wet with her need. The wool felt rough and scratchy through the thin silk of her panties.

Desperate for release, shy ground her hips into his.

"Go on, sweetheart," he urged her.

Shy opened her eyes and looked into his, dark with passion.

Passion for her.

Undone by his desire, she threw her head back as her climax started to take her over, one heavy pulse of pleasure at a time.

His mouth found the wildly beating pulse in her neck. One hand found her clit, hard and throbbing, the other her aching nipples.

One touch, then two and she was completely lost, exploding against him, and then somehow her legs were around his waist and he was sliding into her, sure and fierce. She found his lips again, wanting to show him how much she loved the way she felt when he was touching her.

"Callie," he groaned, her name sounding

like worship, and all of her visions from the sleepless night before merged with their sweaty sex in the refrigerator and the tequila shots and her rubbing herself in the shower dreaming of Derek.

Her inner muscles clenched around his cock and she cried out into his mouth, his tongue pumping in and out of her mouth in the same rhythm that he was thrusting into her.

"Miss Callie?"

A small voice from the hallway was calling out her name and Callie tried to get her brain, her mouth, to respond, but Derek got there first.

"Callie will be out in a minute."

Her legs were shaky and she felt so helpless all of a sudden that she stood completely still while Derek righted her clothes.

Pushing her hair back from her face and tucking it behind her ears, he said, "You blow my mind, sweetheart."

Callie blushed at her out-of-control need for him and bent down to pick up his jacket so that she wouldn't have to look him in the eye. She handed it to him and he quickly threw his condom in the trash, then rearranged his own clothes, stepping back from the door to give Callie room to open it.

Jonah, a ten–year-old whose mother

owned a gift shop on the other end of Main Street, poked his woolen capped head into the storeroom.

He beamed when he saw Callie.

"My mom needs a box of truffles for her store and she sent me over here to see if you could give me some before we open. I sure am glad you're here or else I'd have to ride my bike all the way down here again later."

Walking through the doorway on shaky legs, she ruffled Jonah on the head.

"Oh no, Jonah. I'd hate for you to have to ride your bike all the way down Main Street. Again."

Callie heard the trembling behind her teasing words and hated herself for it. She was sure that Derek could hear it too.

Why, she wondered, couldn't she be calm, cool, and collected around him? Why did she have to be so pathetically attracted to him?

On the way into the front of her shop, she grabbed her jacket from her office chair, wishing she had stayed with her plan of keeping it on, no matter what.

If she had known she was meeting with Derek she would have worn her most chaste outfit, something from the back of closet that covered every square inch of skin from her chin to her ankles.

Callie closed the one button at the waist and wondered how she could have ever possibly felt stern and business-like. This suit was, she now realized, as good as wearing a sign that said, "Fuck me, please. I like sex with men I don't know."

What she wouldn't give for a coat of armor now.

She pulled a large chocolate box off of the shelf and handed it to Jonah. "Why don't you pick out your favorites, honey?" she said, knowing that her hands would be shaking so hard she'd barely be able to get the truffles into the box.

Jonah gave her a look of surprise, but quickly stripped off his mittens and got to work loading up mint and dark chocolate truffles into the box. Even as she chose a lollipop for Jonah from her stash of goodies below the cash register, Callie was far too aware of Derek's large, hot presence behind her.

Everything about him radiated power and sex, all of the stuff she had always been a sucker for.

Look what being a sucker for big, hard men had gotten her so far, she reminded herself harshly. She was alone and nearly broke, with nothing but a failing candy store and a furry mutt to keep her company.

"Miss Callie, I'm done now," Jonah said, snapping her out of her self-pity. "Here," he said, putting a $20 bill in Callie's hand.

She put the bill away in the cash register then handed the little boy his special treat.

"My favorite!" he exclaimed as he shoved the lollipop into the pocket of his down jacket. "Thanks, Miss Callie," he added, getting on his tippy toes to give her a peck on the cheek before he ran out of the heated store into the cold and shot back down Main Street on his bike.

Her heart swelled with affection. What she wouldn't give to have a child of her own.

"Cute kid," Derek said, walking around the front of her display counters to check out her displays.

Callie jumped. *Enough is enough*, she told herself firmly, her heart fluttering just because of Derek's intense presence in her store. She needed to focus on business, not pleasure.

She needed The Candy King to do more than make her come. She needed him to help her save her store.

"Do you always give away candy like that?" Derek's tone was light, but she sensed an edge behind his words

"Of course I do," she replied. She hated that she felt like she needed to explain herself, but she said, "Kids love getting a little surprise."

He stopped his perusal of her storefront. "And you like to give sweet surprises, don't you?" he asked, pinning her with his hot gaze.

She swallowed convulsively, but her mouth felt dry and her tongue refused to fit within the confines of her mouth. All she could do was nod.

The silence between them in Callie's Candies was almost a live being. She wished she knew what happened to her when Derek was near, that way she might have had a chance in hell at fighting it.

But when he finally said, "I like that about you, Callie. I like that a lot. I like everything about you," she knew she was irrevocably lost.

"Lock the door," she said, then turned and walked back into her storeroom.

She heard the lock click shut and undid the button on her jacket. Shrugging out of the pink wool, she threw it onto her desk.

She reached for the zipper on her skirt just as Derek walked through the door and let it drop to the floor.

Standing before Derek in her see-through white silk camisole and white silk thong panties, she said, "One more time. And then we'll take care of business."

Chapter Seven

"Remind me again," Callie said as she stamped her feet in the snow to stay warm. "Why are we doing this?"

Derek put the huge cooler he had been carrying into the snow on the edge of the rink. "Ice skaters love two things," he said, taking a moment to admire how cute Callie looked in her form fitted pink down jacket and tight black ski pants. "Perfect ice, obviously, and, even more importantly, chocolate."

Callie humphed and rubbed her mittened hands together. "If I weren't so cold I might care."

Derek wanted to suck that pouty lower lip of Callie's into his mouth.

It really was too bad that after leaving Callie's Candies on Monday, after their crazy, perfect sex on the steel kitchen island in the middle of her store's back kitchen, Derek felt he had to make the only decision possible under the circumstances—to back off until Callie's Candies was back in the black and running smoothly.

It was perfectly all right to fuck Callie's brains out before they discussed business, but once the first professional word had been spoken, Derek knew not touching Callie was the right thing to do.

Not, of course, that he would hesitate to rip her clothes off and keep her naked in his bed for a week once their business transaction had ended.

But for the time being, the last thing Derek wanted was for Callie to think that the success of her business was in any way linked to whether or not she put out. For the past fifteen years he had been the consummate professional with his clients. He didn't mix business with pleasure, although, truth be told, he had never been tempted to lick cocoa powder off one of his clients before.

In any case, given that this was his last job in the candy business before the world of accounting took him in, he felt an even greater motivation to do his very best.

Not to mention the fact that he had a very strong personal interest in his gorgeous, talented client.

He was going to stick to his decision. Even if it killed him.

Looking at the way Callie's ass rounded up at him as she bent over to unlatch the cooler, Derek was pretty damn sure that keeping his hands off the delectable little candy maker was, indeed, going to destroy him.

After their meeting on Monday, Derek had spent the week holed up in his office, working up a plan of money-making action for her. After looking through her books, he saw that although she was doing fairly well in sales, she was in such a high-rent district that she'd have to either move to another town or double her daily sales.

Their conversation on this matter had been short and sweet.

Derek: "Have you thought about moving to another location?"

Callie: "No."

Derek: "The rent is lower and you wouldn't have to worry about losing your shop."

Callie: "I grew up here and I'm staying here. Isn't it your job to figure out a way to make that work?"

Derek grinned. Just looking at Callie, all small and round and pink, her fiery, sharp mind wasn't inherently obvious. But it was there.

Along with her ravenous sensuality.

Plans for saving Callie's Candies consumed him. He'd already had a web site built for her at a reduced rate by his sister-in-law, who was one of the best in the business, by promising her all the truffles she could eat for the next decade. He was doing the same trade with a hot public relations firm. Next week, he was going to look into national distribution through major gourmet food chain stores.

In any normal consultation situation, Derek would have met with her again in person to run his ideas by her, but the truth was that he knew he wouldn't be able to control himself around her.

Somewhat wryly, he admitted that he might as well have met with Callie in person, considering that even though they had been apart for nearly a week, he had been constantly possessed by visions of her.

Naked thighs and breasts spread across satin sheets. In the shower with soap suds dripping from her nipples.

He forcefully shook the visions from his head and went to work unrolling the new banner that spelled out *www.calliescandies.com*.

He hung it from the roof of the gazebo where they were setting up shop. The gazebo was situated on the far edge of the large outdoor ice skating rink in Saratoga, less than a mile from the world famous racetracks. Based on his experience of taking his nieces and nephews skating over the years, he knew that on Saturdays and Sundays in January, the rink was packed with kids of all ages and their parents, the perfect audience to spread the word about Callie's incredible confections.

"I'm still not sure about the web site," Callie said. "Wouldn't people rather come into the store?"

Feeling incredibly protective towards his luscious client, Derek wanted to allay her fears. "You've got a great store, Callie. It's warm and inviting and who can resist your little surprises?"

Derek saw the responsive spark in Callie's eyes and caught himself just in time before he lost sight of business altogether.

Focus, buddy. Focus.

"What about people who don't live in Saratoga and can't get to your store on a regular basis?"

Callie looked confused. "How would they even find out about my store in the first place?"

"You see all of these people out here today?" Derek asked, gesturing to the growing crowd of skaters that were sliding across the ice. "People are willing to drive quite a distance to skate at such a great outdoor rink. Not to mention the fact that locals often have friends or relatives visiting them for the holidays from out of town."

"And you think these people will love my truffles and hot cocoa so much that they'll want to order more from my web site when they get home?"

"Exactly," Derek said, pleased that Callie was letting herself be open to the array of possibilities for her business.

"I never would have thought to do any of this without you. The web site. Being here today. Getting plans together for a special Valentine's Day gift box."

"It's my pleasure," he said, his voice husky with need.

The only way he could keep himself from dragging her against him and kissing her was to turn and start pulling boxes of truffles out of the cooler for their sales table.

Even during their brief phone calls, he had gotten so overheated he'd had to walk out of his office in just his shirt and slacks until the cold weather had frozen him completely through.

Only then could he concentrate on

business again.

Thirty minutes later, just before the doors to the rink opened up to the crowd that had gathered in the parking lot outside, they'd finished setting up the Callie's Candies booth, complete with steaming hot cocoa and truffles in ten different flavors.

Callie had packed toffees, taffies and lollipops into small wicker baskets on the table.

They took a few steps back to check over their candy display.

"It looks great," Callie said, not quite meeting his eyes.

Derek nodded and smiled at the top of her head. "It certainly does. The table is colorful and inviting. I'm certain that Callie's Candies is going to make a huge splash with both the locals and the out-of-towners today."

Callie walked back to the table and fussed needlessly with the display. Derek could tell that she was feeling nervous around him.

It was taking every ounce of control for Derek to keep his mind on business, when all he really wanted to do was strip off Callie's winter clothes. It was so cold he was starting to add intense visions about hot tubs and saunas to his previous beach and bikini fantasies.

Not for the first time that day, Derek gave thanks that they were conducting their business together in the frigid outdoors. He didn't think he could keep himself from tearing her clothes off if they were alone and indoors. Even as it was, the cold wasn't working its magic on his overcharged libido.

Callie's pull was just too damn strong.

* * * * *

Callie looked at her watch and prayed that her twelve-year-old niece would show up already. She had asked Ellen to help them sell candy as a buffer. Being alone with Derek was harder than she had ever thought it would be. And she had thought that it was going to be pretty hard.

He was so dark and tall and gorgeous, her breath caught in her chest every time she looked at him.

She wanted to drag him behind a tree and pull him down onto the fresh snow with her.

But it didn't matter what Callie wanted. Simply put, the facts were not in her favor.

Fact: He was her hired consultant. It would be morally wrong for her to engage in sexual acts with one of her employees. Under no circumstances did she want him to feel that he had to sleep with her or else she'd bad mouth him in the candy industry.

Fact: Given the fact that he hadn't come near her since Monday when she given herself to him on the stainless steel counter top in her store's kitchen, she'd had to face the painful truth that he wasn't the least bit interested in her anymore. Which meant the high and mighty morals she was desperately trying to cling to didn't matter for much at all.

Even his phone calls had been oh-so-brief, as if he could hardly stand to talk to her again. Every time she thought about the way she had stuck her tongue down his throat in her store, with absolutely no provocation on his part, when she remembered the way she had stripped off her clothes and begged him to touch her, Callie felt more and more embarrassed.

"Aunt Callie, I'm here."

Callie spun around and hugged her little teenage salvation a little too hard.

"Ouch."

"Sorry, honey. I'm just so glad to see you."

Ellen raised an eyebrow, looking far older than thirteen. "Yeah. Whatever. Hey," she said, elbowing Callie in the ribs, "who's the guy? Your new boyfriend?"

Callie turned a hundred shades of pink. "No," she insisted, but Derek was already making the introductions.

"I'm Derek," he said, as he reached out his hand to shake Ellen's. "I've been working with Callie on her business. I'm a candy company consultant."

Ellen smiled and then looked back at Callie. "That's cool. I'm Ellen."

Callie thought she was off the hook, but then Ellen added, "I thought you were her new boyfriend or something, 'cause she always goes for guys who look like you."

Derek grinned and trapped Callie with his hot gaze before turning back to Ellen for more information.

"So Callie likes guys who look like me, huh?"

Ellen shrugged. "Big. Brown hair. Lots of muscles. They usually treat her like dirt, though, so I guess it's a good thing you aren't her boyfriend after all."

Not realizing that she'd said anything out of line at all, Ellen turned to Callie, "So, what do you need me to do?"

Callie was having trouble keeping on her feet at that moment, so she certainly couldn't open up her mouth to reply.

Derek, bless his sinfully gorgeous heart, stepped in and saved her.

"We need your help selling candy and hot cocoa. Make sure that you tell everyone who buys something about the web site and hand them one of Callie's cards."

Ellen nodded. "That sounds easy." She looked up and saw the web site address on the banner. "When did you get a web site, Callie? I'll check it out when I get home. You're practically gonna be famous now."

But Ellen's earlier words wouldn't stop playing in her head. *They usually treat her like dirt, so I guess it's a good thing you aren't her boyfriend after all.*

Was she really that bad at choosing men?

The doors to the rink opened and within a matter of minutes, Callie, Derek and Ellen were swarmed with skaters. People started with the hot chocolate, but after they exclaimed with rapture over the exotic flavor of Callie's cocoa and inquired about purchasing the mix to take home, people turned to truffles and toffee and taffy.

Derek made several trips to Callie's car as their boxes of backup supplies quickly disappeared. Between bites of candy and sips of cocoa, Callie heard snippets of conversation.

"Did you know that she has a web site?"

"I'm going to tell all of my friends out in California about her."

"This is the best truffle I've ever had. I

wonder if she does gift baskets?"

Between sales Callie stole glances at Derek. Her breath went as she watched him joke with the customers. He was so warm and engaging, he had everyone eating out of his hands.

He had most certainly earned his Candy King title. His love for candy came through in everything he did and his quick mind and charming personality sealed the deal.

It was too bad he obviously didn't want to kiss her again. Because she couldn't think of anything she wanted to do more.

* * * * *

Several hours later, when the initial crowds had finally died down and Callie was busy mixing up a new batch of hot cocoa, Derek whispered to Ellen, "Can you hold down the fort for a little while? Your Aunt Callie didn't want to leave you here all alone, but she's been dying to go ice skating with me. And you've been doing the best job out of the three of us. I know a natural when I see one."

Ellen nodded, clearly pleased to be left in charge of the Callie's Candies booth.

"Sure thing, Derek," she whispered back. "By the way, I think Aunt Callie kind of likes you."

"Really?" he whispered back, enjoying the conspiracy. "What makes you say that?"

"Every time she looks at you she gets all dreamy eyed."

Derek grinned and started to get up, but Ellen grabbed the elbow of his jacket.

"You're not gonna break her heart too, are you?"

Derek sat back down, suddenly serious. "I don't intend to."

Ellen stared him down and he was surprised by the intensity in her young eyes.

"Promise? 'Cause I really like you."

Callie's niece sure loved her, Derek thought, to be giving out such stern warnings to prospective boyfriends. His face solemn, he said, "I promise. And I really like you too."

Ellen grinned and turned to greet a new customer who had just walked up to the table. Derek waited until Callie put the top back on her metal pot of cocoa and then grabbed her hand.

"What's going on?" she asked, trying to pull her hand back out of his. "Where are we going?"

Over his shoulder he said, "It's time for a little break, Miss Callie."

"A break? Now? But what about Ellen?"

"Ellen's got it covered. Now tell me," he said, "What size are you?"

Callie flushed and looked down at her chest. "What size am I? What kind of a question is that?"

"What size shoe do you wear?"

"Six, but what does it have to do with…"

Her words fell away as he let go of her hand and picked up one set of rental skates in a six for her and twelve for himself.

Dangling the skates from his fingertips he said, "You and I are going skating."

Callie shook her head. "I don't think so."

Derek grabbed her hand again and steered her over to a bench. "Put 'em on. Consultant's orders."

She reluctantly took the skates from him. Staring at them, she said, "I haven't skated in years."

"No time like the present," he said, as he quickly removed his shoes and slipped his feet into the skates. "Besides, you deserve a reward for all of your hard work today."

He hoped Callie would let herself have a little fun. With him.

He saw her shoulders relax a little and breathed out an inaudible sigh of relief. And when she shot him her pixie grin, he made a new decision—to forget all about his earlier decision about not mixing business with pleasure.

If ever there was a time for pleasure, it was now.

And by god, he was going to take it.

Chapter Eight

Callie had just finished tying the laces on her skates when Derek whirled her out onto the crowded ice skating rink. Her legs wobbled beneath her and she found herself holding on to him just a little too tightly.

"I need to get my skating legs back," she said by way of explanation, letting herself enjoy the feel of his warmth pressed up against hers while she could. He had one arm firmly wrapped around her waist and she could feel his warm breath on her forehead. His arms were heaven.

"No rush," he said, pulling her closer.

They skated several circles around the rink in a comfortable rhythm and for the first time all day Callie let down her guard.

Suddenly, Derek steered them over to the far, deserted edge of the rink and pointed to the sky. "Did you see that bald eagle over there?"

"Where?" She shaded her eyes with her hands, but all she could see on the pine trees was white powder from the fresh snowfall.

"In the forest. Come with me."

Derek grabbed her hand and pulled her into the dense forest with him. Her skates sank into the snow, but he was moving so fast, she didn't have a chance to get stuck as she tried to keep up.

By the time he stopped, they were far enough from the skating rink that the sounds of children playing had completely faded away. Not letting go of her hand, he turned and looked into her eyes.

"I guess he flew away."

Callie found herself laughing. "Was there really a bald eagle out here?"

Derek pulled her into him and leaned his face down close to hers. "Maybe there was, but all I've been able to focus on today is you."

She breathed in his scent, unable to mask the raw need his words aroused. "Don't tease me, Derek."

"Not even if it makes you feel good?"

"How good?"

Callie felt the familiar liquid rush building up between her legs, pooling at the tip of her breasts.

"Really, really good."

He guided her over to a patch of ground far beneath the huge canopy of an oak tree and pressed her back into the bark of the tree, then leaned into her, shielding her from the cold.

"One day we're going to do this properly. Warm and cozy in bed."

Callie shivered at the thought of getting to do this with Derek one more time. In a bed, even. It was too delicious to believe. But then again so was the velvet feel of his lips as they stole her breath away.

Feeling bold, she said between kisses, "I like being crazy, being bad with you."

He smiled against her lips. "Me too, sweetheart. I love the way you wrap your legs around me. How slick you get when I'm pumping in and out of you. How ready you are for me all the time."

She swallowed and licked her lips. "I'm ready now," she whispered.

Deftly he threw his gloves to the ground and unbuttoned the fly on her snow pants. Unzipping them, he slid his warm hands onto the soft skin of her belly, just grazing the edge of her already damp mons.

"Mmm," he murmured against her ear lobe, sucking it into his mouth, "you are ready, aren't you?"

The feel of his mouth against her brought goose bumps to her skin that had nothing to do with the cold. She arched her hips into his hands, forcing his fingers to slide across her swollen nub into her wet folds.

"I want to see you come again, Callie."

He made several slow, torturous circles on her clit and then slipped his fingers down into her labia, finally pushing her open with one thick finger.

Callie drove her hips into his hand.

"Come for me, sweetheart," he said against her lips and Callie, who wanted to please him more than anything else in the world, felt everything inside and outside go perfectly still, as if the whole universe was waiting for her to explode.

Derek looked into her eyes and one simple word, "Now," was all it took.

She closed her eyes as the earth starting spinning fast, too fast. She came out of her body and lifted higher and higher. Everything turned red, then black, as pleasure coursed through her. And then she was kissing him and he was kissing her back, their lips mating in perfect rhythm to her waves of ecstasy.

Derek quickly stripped off his winter coat and laid it on the ground, seemingly impervious to the cold. Gently, he lowered Callie onto it.

She lay back on her elbows and looked at him, excitement making her breath come out in short, quick white puffs of air.

"I wish I could take off all of your clothes and see you naked," he said as he pulled her pants and soaked panties down far enough to spread her thighs.

"Later," she said, not feeling the least bit inhibited about lying in the snow in the forest, naked from her waist to her ankles.

"Later," he echoed as he bent his head over her mound, lapping at her sweetness with his tongue.

Callie arched up into his mouth. She felt like she could come and come and come and come and it still wouldn't take the edge off her arousal.

He slipped his tongue inside of her in one firm, long stroke and then another. Callie gasped and her muscles clenched around his tongue. His thumb found her clit and She cried out as her orgasm ripped through her, the sound muted by the thick canopy of the pine tree. Derek replaced his tongue with two fingers and sucked her clit into his mouth, faster and faster, harder and harder. She writhed beneath him, her fingers tangled in his thick brown hair.

She was tumbling through space, dizzy with pleasure as he reared up over her, pushing her thighs open just a little more so that he could kneel between her legs.

Callie opened her eyes and saw his perfect cock, so hard and pushing out from his dark pubic hair, already sheathed within a condom.

She wanted to reach out her hand to stroke him, to fill her small hand with the heavy weight of his shaft, but before she could even think about taking off her gloves, he was unzipping her coat and running his hands over her turtleneck, teasing her taut peaks.

"Squeeze your thighs together," he said.

Callie barely managed to obey him, she was so concentrated on the feel of Derek over her. On her. In her.

She wrapped her hands around his shoulders to pull him closer while she squeezed her thighs together as tight as she could.

She felt his cock growing impossibly bigger within her with every stroke and suddenly she was floating and he was coming and saying her name and she was moving with him, bucking her hips up off the blanket of his jacket, trying to get closer to him, as close as she could possibly get.

* * * * *

Afraid of crushing her, Derek tried to prop his weight up on his forearms, but she was holding him so tightly to her that he decided to just let himself go.

He rolled them over slightly, so that he was cradling her in his arms, their bodies still joined together. The truth hit him like a bolt of lightning.

He was in love with her.

He had never been so sexually compatible with any woman, but it was more than just the incredible sex that made him so positive that Callie was the one.

She was funny and bright and just seeing her smile made him want to do or say something to make her smile again.

Her breathing began to slow to normal and he rubbed her back, savoring the feeling of having found the woman he wanted to spend the rest of his life with.

They needed to get back to the rink, but he didn't want to move too fast back to real life. He slowly pulled out and zipped his pants back up.

Callie blinked and then fumbled for her snow pants. Pulling her to her feet, Derek took care of getting her back in order within seconds.

He took her face in his hands and kissed her, long and slow and sweet.

"This isn't a one-night stand," he said, his voice firm and tender all at the same time.

Callie smiled back at him and covered his hands with her own.

"I know."

Chapter Nine

The next two weeks were the best of Callie's life. After their incredible lovemaking in the forest, they had gone back to the rink to pack up her sales table. Much to her surprise, Derek had insisted that they talk about their relationship. She had never met a man like him before, one who was willing to broach difficult subjects. Every man she'd ever known before had hidden from emotions, had ignored anything that wasn't cut and dry.

"I want to date you," he said, and she said, "Me too."

"I know I'm working for you," he said, and she said, "And I've hired you."

"I want to be your lover as well as your business associate," he said, and she said, "Thank god."

They had both laughed and suddenly the

air was clear and full of endless possibilities.

Not only was Callie constantly glowing with joy, but her business was growing by leaps and bounds as well, with a huge spike in business from Internet orders.

One night after a romantic dinner at her house where they had done more hand-holding and kissing than eating, Callie said, "You really are the Candy King, you know," her tone teasing.

Derek stiffened slightly at her words, but then relaxed again so quickly she was certain that she had imagined it.

"How did you know that you were so darn good at selling candy?"

Derek kissed her on her neck, right below her ear, in just the way that was guaranteed to make her nipples hard and aching.

"You don't want to hear about my boring business," he said, trying to coax her into another incredible sexual interlude, his palm coming to cup her between her thighs, searing her with his heat even through her jeans.

But even though she was already responding to his touch, her breasts heavy, her mons throbbing, Callie'd had enough of his putting her off. Last night after making love in her bathtub, she had finally realized that whenever she asked him questions about his company, he deftly changed the subject. Usually by kissing or touching her, until she was naked and coming beneath him, all thoughts of business gone.

Callie scooted away from Derek on the couch, hating how empty she felt without his touch, but knowing they needed to have this conversation more than they needed to have sex.

"Why do you keep pushing my questions away?"

Derek looked at the empty place on the couch where she'd been just seconds before. "What are you talking about?"

She sighed. "Every time I bring up your business, you change the subject. For the past two weeks all we've talked about is Callie's Candies." Her voice softened. "I want to find out more about you, Derek."

He looked so tense she had to scoot back into the circle of his arms and plant several kisses on his forearms and hands, pulling his strong arms around her.

His muscles relaxed slightly. But still, he didn't offer her any information about his past.

Trying to hide her growing exasperation, she said, "What was your favorite kind of candy when you were a kid?"

"Necco Wafers."

Sticking her tongue out, Callie

scrunched her face up. "Yuck."

"They're sweet and sort of chalky," he whispered in her ear. "Just like somebody I know, minus the chalk of course. You're all sweetness."

Callie sucked in a breath as his fingers moved to the curve of her breast. It was taking everything she had not to forget the whole conversation and just make love to him. She could feel his large erection pushing into her bottom, and she wriggled up against him.

"Please, Derek, talk to me."

Callie had always thought that patience was one of her strong suits—after all, she dealt with children as customers on a daily basis—but in the silence that ensued, where all she could hear was the crackling wood on the fire and Wolf's heavy dog breathing, she realized how wrong she was.

She was about to give up on ever finding anything out about Derek's past when his hand stilled on her breast.

"I worked for Mr. Jonas after school at his grocery store. He had a small candy section in the corner and he put me in charge of it."

Aha, now they were getting somewhere. "Free candy?"

Derek grinned against the top of her head and he scooted her in more snugly against his lap. "All I could eat. I started arranging things differently, putting up new signs, created some package deals, and by the time I graduated from high school, Mr. Jonas's candy store was about ten times bigger."

"And then?"

"And then I went to college, got an MBA with a focus in food retailing, and the rest," he said with a note of finality, "is history. Now let's get back to the good stuff."

Callie reached up to lace her fingers into his thick dark hair. Pressing her lips to his, she kissed him with all of the growing love in her heart.

She wasn't ready to say the words to him yet, but every time she touched him she knew that her feelings were obvious.

"Thank you for telling me all that," she said, her lips bruised with their passionate kisses.

Derek leaned down and licked her full lower lip. "You're welcome, sweetheart."

Callie shivered. She loved it when he called her sweetheart. Even though they'd only been formally dating for two weeks, she felt closer to him than she ever had to another person. She had shared her body and soul with Derek and somewhere in the back of her head she knew she wanted to continue doing so for the rest of her life.

She was so relaxed and content in his arms that when he said, "Now is probably a good time to tell you that I'm closing my business and going to work with my brother," she jumped with surprise. The top of her head knocked into his chin, clacking his teeth together.

She spun out of his arms. "You're doing what?"

Derek's face turned from loving to grim in the space of a heartbeat.

"You're my last client."

Callie forgot all about being supportive and gentle in her shock. "Why would you do something like that?"

His eyes steel, he said, "It's time to finally grow up."

"What are you talking about? You have a wonderful business. And from working with you, I know for a fact that you love what you do." She narrowed her eyes. "What are you planning to do instead?"

Derek nearly winced. "Accounting."

Callie's eyes grew wide. "Excuse me? I must have heard you wrong. I thought my talented, creative boyfriend just said he's going to give up his dream job to go into accounting."

Derek got up off the couch. "You heard

right. My brother Jed is going to bring me into his department."

His voice was hard and Wolf, who was lying on the rug in front of the roaring fireplace, whined.

"I've got some work to take care of. I'll call you later." He walked out the front door and closed it behind him with a deliberate click.

The tears that were welling in Callie's eyes started to fall. Wolf got up and padded over to her, licking her face several times before plopping his head on her lap.

"I've really blown it this time, Wolf," she said, her heart heavy.

She scooted out from underneath Wolf's head, then walked into her kitchen and pulled out the ingredients for cocoa fudge. She knew she wouldn't be able to sleep tonight, not for one single minute, not with the distressed look on Derek's face playing in her head on repeat every five seconds. The only thing that would keep her from going crazy would be baking.

She wiped at the tears on her cheeks and put on her apron.

"Here I am again," she said aloud in her empty kitchen. "Just me, my dog, and sugar."

Chapter Ten

The next day Derek walked into Callie's Candies holding a bright bouquet of yellow and white narcissus. She was down on the ground with her back to the front door, helping two little girls pick out a gift for their mother's birthday while their father watched with pride.

"Mommies love these boxes of truffles," she said to the girls as she showed them a heart shaped box with a thick velvet ribbon on top.

The two girls solemnly nodded their agreement and handed her a five dollar bill. Just as solemnly, treating them as if they were adults buying thousands of dollars of merchandise instead of little kids, Callie took their money and walked around to her register.

Derek noted that her eyes and face looked swollen and puffy and inwardly cursed himself. He had done that to her with his callous, selfish behavior.

He felt a deep sense of shame at the way he had treated Callie.

She had called him her boyfriend, a word that made him feel better than any industry award ever had, and he had stomped out of her home in a huff.

Idiot.

He was surprised by her reaction to his planned career change. Any other woman would have applauded his move into a serious business.

But Callie wasn't like anyone else.

She looked up and saw him standing awkwardly by the door, holding the flowers as an obvious peace offering, and nearly dropped the box of truffles on the floor. She caught the box in mid-air and placed it on her gift-wrapping table, her hands shaky.

She gave him a tremulous smile and was about to say something when Derek smiled back and leaned against the wall, making it clear that he could wait until she was done helping the girls.

She finished wrapping the truffles with trembling fingers. She handed the girls a lollipop each and then followed them with her eyes as they took their father's hand and skipped out the door.

Derek approached her at the same time

that she ran around the counter. Their words intermingled, "I'm so sorry," he said, and she said, "No, I'm the one who's sorry."

He handed her the bouquet and she clutched the flowers to her chest as if they were more valuable to her than gold or diamonds.

"Can you forgive me?"

He stroked her cheek with his fingers. "What did I ever do right to deserve you?"

She shook her head. "I'm the lucky one. And I want you to know that I'll always support you. Whatever you do, I'll still love you."

She gasped and backed into the counter, dropping the flowers onto the floor, her hands moving her mouth in shock.

She loved him.

Thanking god, Derek closed the space between them, stepping into the circle of flowers on the floor.

"I love you too."

Burying his hands in Callie's soft hair, he dipped his mouth to hers and tasted her sweetness. Her hands wrapped around him and she pulled him tightly to her. Even the bell ringing on the door to the shop, indicating that a customer had entered, was not enough for either of them to want to pull away from each other.

"Ahem," a firm voice said from behind Derek's back.

He pulled away from Callie's sweet lips and groaned, knowing that voice could only belong to one person.

Looking over his shoulder he said, "Hello, Alice."

Shaking her head as if they were two kids goofing around during class, Alice said, "I thought I might find you here."

Callie slid out from Derek's arms and held out her hand, looking charmingly disheveled.

"I've been so looking forward to meeting you, Alice." Callie blushed. "Under different circumstances, of course."

Alice yielded slightly under the weight of Callie's charm and shook her hand.

Turning back to Derek, the older woman said, "I'd like to know if you think your behavior is going to sell more candy in this store, or less? You've got an important meeting in five minutes at the office."

Derek grinned shamelessly and held his hands up in defeat. "Point taken, sergeant."

He leaned over the counter and placed another quick kiss on Callie's lips. "Are we still on for dinner tonight? My family has been dying to meet you."

Callie whispered, "I can't wait," and they made do with one more quick peck.

She stood in the store alone with Alice, feeling more nervous than she had since she was a schoolgirl. But Derek's assistant wasn't one to beat around the bush.

"I'll get straight to the point."

Callie nodded, her heart pounding even though she hadn't done anything wrong. Trying to break the ice, Callie interrupted and said, "Can I offer you anything first? Maybe some hot cocoa and a truffle?"

Alice looked momentarily flustered. "Why yes," she said. "I could use a hot drink to warm my bones."

Callie went to pour her a steaming cup and Alice said, "And if you wouldn't mind, I'd love a truffle. I had one last year and I still haven't forgotten it."

Callie breathed a sigh of relief. Derek's assistant seemed a whole lot less scary when she had chocolate smudged on her lips.

"I didn't mean to interrupt you," she said, after Alice had bitten into the truffle with a sound of delight.

Alice held up her hand, making it clear that she wanted to finish the chocolate in silence. Callie grinned, pleased that her candy made people so happy.

But her grin fell away as the woman said, "I wasn't sure that I approved of your relationship with Derek at first—it is unprofessional for a consultant to date his client, after all—but now I can see that you're the best thing that's happened to him in some time."

Callie was frozen where she stood.

"I love him like a son and he's about to make the biggest mistake of his life. I want you to stop him."

Callie's brain struggled to catch up. "Do you mean how he's closing his business?"

Alice nodded, her lips tight again in disapproval.

"Has he talked to you about it?"

"No. But that boy can't hide anything from me. Never could, never will. I've known for months. But I also know that he hasn't made it official yet by firing me because he doesn't really want to shut down his dreams."

"Alice, I appreciate you coming here to try and help Derek, but I don't think he's going to listen to me."

Alice's eyes were bright. "Honey, that's where you're wrong. You could tell him to jump off of a cliff and he'd do it. It's up to you to make sure he doesn't make the biggest mistake of his life. I'm counting on you."

* * * * *

That night as Callie sat in the chic new restaurant surrounded by Derek's parents and his brother and wife, she was still trying to get Alice's words out of her head.

He doesn't want to do it. It's up to you to make sure he doesn't make the biggest mistake of his life. I'm counting on you.

Callie tried to focus on getting to know Derek's relatives, all the while wondering when things had become so complicated. One day she was running a very small business and the next she was dating a passionate, complex man who was turning both her little store and her life upside down.

Derek's mother, Joan, turned to her and said, "So you're the famous Callie from Callie's Candies?"

She blushed. "I don't know about famous."

Joan waved her hand in the air. "Nonsense. My women's group has been enjoying your truffles for years. And besides," she said, lowering her voice, "John and I haven't heard about anything else for weeks."

Callie stuttered unintelligible monosyllables, but Joan obviously wasn't expecting a response.

"John and I think it is just perfect that you and Derek found each other. Two candy lovers who are obviously in love with each other."

Callie had to clamp her teeth together to keep her mouth from falling open. She tried to smile, but she was sure her attempt looked pathetic. Thankfully, Joan was drawn into a conversation with her husband and Derek. Callie turned to Derek's older brother, Jed, with relief.

Jed leered at her and she barely repressed a shudder as she took in his beady eyes, oily hair, and bad breath. His wife, a thin dour woman, sat like a mouse beside him. Her eyes were glassy and Callie didn't envy the woman one bit.

"So you own a candy store," he said, more a statement than a question.

"That's right. Callie's Candies is just down the street."

Derek's brother rolled his eyes. "Candy," he scoffed. "Good thing my brother has finally come to his senses."

Callie sucked in a breath. "Excuse me?" she said, her voice soft and still, working hard not to betray her growing anger.

How could it be, she wondered, that Derek and Jed were related by blood? They were polar opposites.

"I've worked on him for years to join me

in the accounting firm. Something he'll finally get some respect for. Do you know how embarrassing it is to be related to the Candy King?" The words 'Candy King' sounded like spoilt milk coming out of Jed's mouth.

Callie curled her fingers tightly into her fist, fighting the overpowering urge to punch Derek's jerk of a brother in his fat mouth.

"No. I don't," she said, deciding her only hope was to humor Jed until dinner was over.

As she nodded in all the right places during Jed's endless discourse on his importance and value as a high-powered accountant, everything became crystal clear to Callie. Jed was jealous of Derek's success and happiness. Obviously, Jed was the one that had been putting pressure on Derek to "finally grow up," since Derek's parents clearly loved and supported him in his career choice. She knew they were proud of him, just as they somehow managed to be proud of their other brute of a son.

A huge weight lifted from her shoulders. She knew what she needed to say to Derek. Maybe, just maybe, she would have a fighting chance at succeeding at convincing him to keep Sweet Returns in business.

Callie planted a smile on her face.

Nothing else Jed said to her tonight was going to bring her down. She would keep up the small talk when she had to and focus most of her attention on getting to know Derek's wonderful parents better.

Whatever she had to put up with to be with Derek was worth it.

* * * * *

Derek sat back and watched Callie charm his family just as she charmed every single person she came in contact with. Even his brother, who could be somewhat standoffish with strangers, was talking animatedly to her.

"Being the VP at an accounting firm is a big responsibility," Jed said, his chest puffed up with pride at his accomplishments.

Derek shook his head as he caught snippets of Jed's conversation with Callie. Derek didn't begrudge his brother any of his success, but sometimes Derek thought he rode the fine line between pride and arrogance.

Thank god Callie didn't care about stuff like that. She just wanted him to be happy.

Callie leaned in towards his brother and said, "Your job sounds really exciting."

Derek blinked hard a couple of times. What the hell was she saying? Jed's job sounded important? And exciting?

His brother said something in response which Derek couldn't hear, but he couldn't miss Callie's impressed response. "That figure was your bonus for last year? Wow. I didn't know accountants did quite so well. Kind of makes me wish I'd been better at math in school," she added with a crooked smile.

Jed's wife finally spoke. "Jed has always provided very well for us."

Callie smiled brightly. "Lucky you."

Suddenly the room felt too small. Derek grabbed at his tie to loosen it from around his neck. As the awful truth crashed in around him, he could no longer breathe.

He shot up out of his chair without a word to anyone and made it as far as the parking lot before he bowled over into a hedge of snow covered boxwood and nearly threw up. He could hardly believe what he had heard, even though now that he had seen the evidence for himself, there was no denying it.

What a fool he'd been. Callie wasn't the woman he thought she was.

Instead of the cute, sweet, supportive woman he thought he loved, instead of the woman who looked at a bouquet of flowers as more precious than jewels, underneath it all she was just as interested in power and money as his ex-fiancée had been.

Derek got in his Ferrari and sped off into the night, leaving behind the woman who had broken his heart in two.

* * * * *

Callie nodded absently at Jed's bragging —he didn't require any help from her to prod his boasting into the stratosphere—wondering where Derek had rushed off to without a word to anyone. When he had been gone more than five minutes, she excused herself and asked the host to check the men's restroom.

Derek was gone.

She slumped into the coat rack, wondering what had happened. One minute everything was great, the next minute her boyfriend was gone.

She went back to the table and asked his parents, "Did Derek say anything to you about needing to leave early?"

His mother and father shook their heads, looking worried. "No. I wonder if something he ate didn't agree with him?"

Callie murmured something that was supposed to be comforting, but her heart wasn't it in. Her boyfriend had walked out on her for the second time in twenty-four hours. She fought back the tears that threatened to spill, not wanting his family to see her looking so pathetic.

Jed, clueless as ever, sneered and said, "Geez. The dumb little brother of mine doesn't even know how to take care of his lady."

Something inside Callie snapped. "You don't know the first thing about your brother," she said and then turned and walked out the restaurant.

He didn't want her.

No man who was worth anything had ever wanted her.

Callie had been dumped before, but this time everything was different.

He had said he loved her. No one had ever said that before.

She took a breath to pull some oxygen into her chest, up into her brain cells.

He'd said *I love you.*

And he'd meant it.

Something must have happened at the restaurant. Something bad enough to make him run.

She was going to find out what it was.

And by god, she was going to fight for him.

And for love.

Chapter Eleven

Callie walked the three blocks to Derek's loft in a driving rain. She didn't care that she was getting soaked to the bone. She didn't care that her teeth were chattering.

Love like this only came once in a lifetime, and no matter what she had to do, or how much of her pride she had to give up, she wasn't going to let it go.

Her hand a tight, frozen fist, she banged on Derek's steel door with all of her might. When he didn't answer immediately, she banged again, using the pain of bone and flesh against metal as a reminder of all that she was fighting for.

Of what she was fighting against.

The rain poured down on the front stoop in sheets and still he didn't answer the door. Intent on waiting for him for as long as it took, Callie slid down to the floor, shivering in her thin sheath dress and heels.

She wrapped her arms tightly around her and rocked back and forth, finally letting the tears that she had been holding back merge with the streaks of rain across her face.

* * * * *

Derek pushed his Ferrari as hard as it would go on the farm roads outside of Saratoga. On a night like this, where the hail was as big as his fist, everyone else had the sense to keep off the roads. Which suited him just fine as he watched his speedometer inch past eighty, then ninety, then one hundred. He drove like a madman, heedless of his own safety, until he skidded to a stop, narrowly missing both a large deer and a deep ditch.

He'd been a fool, not once but twice.

Only, Callie's betrayal cut him a million times deeper than anything else ever had.

Gripping the wheel tightly, he skidded back onto the road, heading for home. He was going to drown his sorrow in anything other than tequila—Derek was never going to drink tequila again, all it did was remind him of Callie's taste—and then he was going to take care of something he had been putting off for too long.

He was going to shut down Sweet Returns.

What did he need with true love and a job he loved? All they'd ever done was cause him trouble.

But when Derek came to a screeching halt in front of his loft, he flew out of his car, unable to believe what he was seeing.

Callie was curled up like a sick child on his front steps, her eyes clenched tightly shut to keep out the rain, her arms and legs covered with red welts from the hail.

His anger forgotten in his fear, he ran to her and picked her up in his arms. Murmuring sounds of comfort into her hair, trying desperately to warm her with his heat, he fumbled with the lock in the door. Finally managing to get it open, he hurried inside and kicked the door shut.

"I'm so cold, Derek. So cold," she said through the loud clacking of her teeth.

Goosebumps covered her skin and he hugged her tighter to him.

"I'm going to run a hot bath for you, sweetheart," he said, the endearment slipping from his lips before he could stop himself.

He'd never stop loving her.

The shock of realization rocked him the rest of the way off his axis. "Once I take these wet clothes off of you, I promise you'll feel better."

She didn't say anything, she just shivered and looked up into his eyes as if she was trying to tell him something important.

But he couldn't let himself think about anything other than getting Callie warm. Otherwise he would have to face anger and pain and hurt so strong he thought he might never laugh or smile again.

Sitting on the wide rim of his large whirlpool tub, still cradling Callie in his lap, he leaned over and turned the knobs until steaming water was pouring into the tub. Quickly, he stripped her dress off and as he undid the clasp of her bra and slid it from her shoulders, he tried not to notice that her nipples were hard buds from the cold. He stripped her panties from her legs and forced himself to ignore how much he wanted to bury his face against her slick heat and taste her one more time.

Gently lowering her into the tub, his hand brushed the soft mound of her breasts and he heard her gasp.

Knowing it was wrong, hating himself for being so out of control, he leaned into her and took one of her nipples in his mouth, suckling hard, wanting to punish and pleasure her in equal parts. She arched up into his mouth, and threaded her fingers into his hair.

With a groan that hid none of his anger at himself or at her, he ripped off his own wet clothes. Callie reached her arms up to him and within seconds he was naked and between her legs.

"I love you, Derek," she cried as her wet, slick canal throbbed around his cock.

He tried to block out her words. He tried to concentrate on the wet warmth that encased his cock, her perfect breasts rubbing against his chest, her round ass in his hands as he pounded in and out of her.

But even as he tried to use her for his pleasure – and nothing else - he couldn't escape the truth.

Cupping her cheeks with his hands, he stilled.

"I love you."

In the space of one heartbeat, they both came apart.

After the madness had subsided, the water sloshed around them in the tub and he pulled away from her.

"Don't leave me again," she said. "We need to talk."

He stood up and water poured off of him into the tub. "Fine," he said, trying to rouse his anger again. "Talk." He grabbed a towel and roughly dried himself off.

She stood up too and grabbed a towel. "Why did you leave the restaurant like that?"

He answered her question with a question. "Why did you lie to me?"

She sat heavily on the rim off the tub, the towel all but forgotten in her hands. "I've never lied to you."

"Bullshit," he said, his eyes flashing dangerously. "I saw the way you were fawning all over my brother." His voice grew high pitched as he imitated her. *"Your job sounds really exciting."* Derek snarled before resuming his parody. *"Wow, I didn't know accountants made so much money."*

Callie gasped in outrage. "How dare you make me sound like…like such a money-grubbing bitch."

He grabbed her by the shoulders, forcing her to stand face to face with him. "Haven't you just been playing at being the nice little candy maker, pretending you wanted me to live my dreams, when all along you just wanted money. And power. Just like Gina."

Callie's fighting stance fell away. "Gina? Who's Gina?"

He let go of her shoulders, trying not to wince at the red marks his fingers had left on her smooth skin.

"My ex."

Callie's voice was soft. "You've never mentioned any ex before."

"She left me at the altar. On the day of our wedding."

Callie took a step closer and put her hand on his arm. "Why?"

He pushed her comfort away with a harsh laugh. "You should understand her motives perfectly. After all, who would want to be married to the Candy King?"

She licked her lips and swallowed once before saying, softly, "I would, Derek."

He turned back to her, anguish etched in the lines of his face. "No, Callie, you don't. You want me to be just like Jed, just like she did. Just like everyone does."

Carefully stepping out of the tub, Callie came toe to toe with Derek. "Your brother is jealous of you. I was stroking his ego in the hopes that he would shut up so that I could get to know your parents better."

"I thought you knew me better than that," she said, her voice shaky. "I thought you knew how much I love you for being you."

Everything in her was telling her to run away, to leave Derek, to give up on them. But she knew it was the coward's way out. She had vowed to fight for their love and now she was being put to the ultimate test.

Callie forced herself to keep talking, hoping that she could keep him from leaving again, hoping that something she said would break down the walls of hurt he had built up long ago.

"I'm not the only one who's proud of you. Your parents are incredibly proud. Alice loves you like a son and it's been killing her to watch you try and shut down something so beautiful that you created from love."

"How do you know these things?"

She reached out a hand to his jaw and was so glad when he didn't push her away. "They all love you, Derek. Just like I do. Even a blind man could see it."

Suddenly, he wrapped his arms around her, dragging her naked breasts against his bare chest.

"What about a stupid man?" he asked, his voice husky yet hopeful.

Tears fell down her cheeks. "Even a stupid man. Especially if he's the most amazing, loving man I've ever met. Now take me to that bed you always talk so much about and love me."

Chapter Twelve

February 14th. Valentine's Day.

Callie opened up her shop and tried not to feel sorry for herself. After all, now that everything was out in the open between her and Derek, she had everything she'd ever dreamed of and more.

She had true love.

She had a man she could talk to about anything, a partner that she could depend on and who could depend on her.

The only thing she didn't have was a date for Valentine's Day.

Again.

Now that Derek was committed to keeping Sweet Returns up and thriving as a candy consulting business, he had been setting up meetings with all of the potential clients that he had put off for the past several months. It just so happened that he had to fly out for an overnight trip to Chicago on Valentine's Day.

He had been incredibly apologetic and Callie had been understanding even though she wanted to beg him to rearrange his schedule.

It was all for the best, she told herself. Valentine's was one of her busiest days of the year and each year, by the time she flipped her sign from open to closed, she could barely do more than drag herself off to bed.

Settling into another "Holiday of Love" at her store, Callie did brisk sales all day. With a smile on her face, she sold out of the expensive gift baskets that Derek had helped her put together and in any spare time she had she filled last-minute orders for chocolate and candy that came in over the Internet.

By 5 p.m. it was dark outside and Callie was exhausted. The big rush was through— most people were at home sharing a romantic evening in front of the fire together by now.

Callie had been hoping that Derek would call and wish her a happy Valentine's Day from Chicago, but every time she picked up her phone it was another customer making an order for a box of truffles or a gift basket.

She was on the phone with a long-distance customer when a delivery truck parked outside her store and a man walked in with a vase of roses.

And then another.

And then another.

Callie quickly wrapped up her call. "Excuse me," she said to the delivery man. "I think you're delivering these roses to the wrong place."

The man looked at his clipboard. "This is Callie's Candies, isn't it?"

Callie nodded, her heart beginning to blossom with joy.

By the time the man drove away, Callie's Candies was filled with vases of roses of every color—on the floor, on the counter, on every shelf. Callie headed for the phone to call Derek's cell phone to thank him for being the most wonderful boyfriend in the world, but before she could wind through the vases of flowers, four men in tuxedos walked through the door carrying musical instruments.

Hardly able to believe what was happening, the string quartet began to serenade her with her favorite symphony.

Tears pooled in her eyes and she had to lean against a display counter to stay steady.

No doubt about it, Derek was the most romantic, wonderful boyfriend in the whole world. Callie couldn't believe she had doubted him for one single second. Even from all the way in Chicago, he was giving her the best

Valentine's Day she had ever had.

And then her heart stopped as the man she loved walked through the door. She ran into Derek's arms and he swept her up against him and kissed her passionately.

"Happy Valentine's Day, sweetheart," he said and she kissed him back with all of the love in her heart.

A few minutes later, the string quartet left.

"I think we're alone now," Derek said in a voice laced with passion and love.

"Lock the door," Callie said, wanting to drag Derek into the back room to rip all of his clothes off and show him just how much his romantic deeds meant to her.

He grinned. "I'm always locking the door when I'm with you."

She planted another kiss on his succulent lips. "That's because I'm always taking off my clothes whenever you're around."

"I knew there was a good reason," he said as he quickly locked the door and pulled down the blinds.

She reached for his big warm hands and pulled him into the back room with her. Propping him up against the door, she dropped to her knees and began to undo his belt loop.

Derek laced his fingers through her hair

and closed his eyes. In seconds, Callie had his hard, throbbing shaft in her greedy fingers.

"Just what I was looking for," she said, as her breath wafted over his pulsating head. "My big, tasty Valentine's Day treat."

Derek groaned as Callie tasted him with the tip of her tongue. She took his length into her mouth, sucking and licking in a perfect rhythm until he couldn't take it anymore.

Dropping to the floor, he had both of their clothes off in record time. Naked, facing each other on their knees, Callie climbed on top of Derek, setting his cock just at the base of her pussy.

"Will you marry me?"

She slid down over him.

"Yes."

Together, they gave each other all of the love they'd been holding deep inside their hearts for so long.

And it was the kind of sweet, passionate love that lasts forever.

~ The End ~